LESSONS

For a

LIFETIME

*Life Lessons of a
Sunday School Teacher*

David Byrd

Unless otherwise noted, all scriptural references are taken from The Thompson Chain-Reference Bible New International Version, Copyright 1983 by The B.B. Kirkbride Bible Company, Inc., Indianapolis, IN 46204, and The Zondervan Corporation, Grand Rapids, MI 49506.

Cover design by Jay Cookingham

ISBN: 0-9769186-5-X

Published by:
Holy Fire Publishing
531 Constitution Blvd. Martinsburg, WV 25401
www.ChristianPublish.com

Printed in the United States of America and the United Kingdom

This book is dedicated to the New Life
Sunday school classes and their members
who have touched my life with perfect love and to
First United Methodist Church
of Waco of which I am so proud.

Contents

Foreword

$\int$ ome years ago, I was looking for just the right person to run one of my businesses. As is my custom, I prayed about this important decision and talked about it with my wife, Jane.

That following Sunday morning, I told Jane, "I want to go to a different church today." It had been five years since we had visited a particular church, but I felt we should go there and visit that Sunday morning.

When we walked in the door, I chose to sit on the left. My usual habit is to sit on the right. As we sat down, I glanced around and saw David Byrd sitting an arm's length away. I said to myself, "This is no coincidence!" David had been involved in an executive capacity with the Meyer family businesses for over twenty years.

I invited him to lunch the next day and offered him the position. He accepted. It was all really quite simple, yet divinely instructed.

Divine instruction has always been a part of David's life. Psalms 37:23 states, "The steps of a good man are ordered by the Lord" (KJV). I know that David operates from that perspective in every area of his life.

As far as my asking David to take the leadership role in my business, it was a very good move indeed! His leadership has been exemplary, and his humility has enabled everyone within the company to grow. The business has grown as well. How can a business not grow when there is a capable servant leader at the helm? The people who work with David are privileged people.

I am confident that you will both enjoy and learn from *Lessons for a Lifetime.* David is an incredible teacher, as well as a Christian brother, business partner, and dear friend. Included in *Lessons for a Lifetime* are many of his revelations, insights, and "talks" with God. These are weighty things brought down to earth through David's comfortable and effective style of communicating.

Lessons for a Lifetime will leave you richer than you know.

Paul J. Meyer
Founder
Leadership Management, Inc.

Introduction

I am a little pencil in the hand of a writing God,
who is sending a love letter to the world.

- Mother Teresa

*B*eginnings usually seem insignificant. Most of us
reflect on our lives as a continuous string of days
filled with memories and give little or no thought to
the cumulative impact of our small starts – our
seemingly insignificant beginnings. However, the
momentum created from those small beginnings
ultimately determines the significance and impact of
our lives. This book is the result of a small start in my
life that transformed into a spiritual mission.

God calls each of us in various ways for different
reasons, and in 1988 He called me to teach an adult
Sunday school class at my church. I still remember the
call from the senior pastor asking me to fill in for an
adult class that was in need of a teacher. I think it is
probably normal, but I began to think of quick
excuses, such as lack of time, job demands, and so on

- all the excuses one contrives when the pressure is on. However, I have always believed that some things happen for a reason, and for reasons unknown at the time, I knew that I could not take this invitation lightly. My response was typical of any red-blooded, moderate layperson: I gave him a six month commitment. "That's the way it works," I told myself. "Step in, grit your teeth, bare the burden, and give it to someone else in six months."

Everyone was very supportive of my new assignment, and the church staff continuously reminded me of what they thought were my "glowing qualifications." But all I could hear was God opening a great big door that seemed far too overwhelming. That was over fifteen years ago. As I reflect on that small start in my life, I realize I had never stopped to think that God was calling me to a life's work – a mission.

When I started teaching, God told me to teach from my heart about real-life issues, to use no other resources or lesson guides – just Him, His word, me, and spiritual insights from real-life experiences. Consistently I have heard God ask me to trust Him for His weekly lesson, and over the years those lessons have become my lessons for a lifetime.

Lesson preparations were difficult in the beginning, but without fail, every Sunday a lesson that always seemed far better than my capabilities would just roll out and be directed at specific, individual needs in the class. My weekly prayer has been, *God, please allow this lesson to be something specific for someone,* and He has faithfully and consistently answered that prayer.

The issue of authority is a looming obstacle for many who are called to teach adult Sunday school. I struggled with this during my first few years of teaching. There seems to be two extremes regarding the issue of authority: Some teachers assume more authority than is justified or necessary, while others underestimate their God-given, unique ability and assume no authority at all. Both of these extremes are limiting and lead some to believe that only clergy has the authority to reveal the nature of God.

However, over time God has taught me a significant lesson about authority. Authority to teach God's word does not generate from one's superior intellect, knowledge, degree(s), or theological understanding. These qualifications are certainly beneficial, but authority to teach comes directly from God. Not all are called to teach in a formal setting, but each person was created to grasp a unique perspective of God's character. We are all called to share, in some way, that unique understanding with the world around us. When I began to observe the common events and insights from my life as spiritual lessons ordained by God, I began to understand that no one else on earth could hold greater authority to teach that unique perspective than I.

For some time now, I have felt led to compile a collection of some of the more popular lessons that I have shared with my Sunday school classes. I have no agenda for this book other than honoring God's call. Truthfully, I have had some conversations with God, questioning His calling me to write this book. I have even visited several Christian book stores attempting to prove to myself, and possibly to God, that there are too many books on the market now addressing the issues of adult Christian education. I told myself, *Surely God would not continue to call this reluctant layman to such an overwhelming task if I could show Him some excellent competition.* But to my surprise, there was not even a section dedicated to adult Christian education in any of the stores I visited. There seems to be a significant gap in the availability of real-life, Spirit-filled lessons for adults that make good common sense.

After God revealed to me the significance of this need, I had no more excuses. I could hear the Spirit's small voice behind me (Isaiah 30:21) saying, "You must write this book." With no excuses, my reluctance began to transform into resolve. This book is the result of God's call and guidance to a reluctant but resolute layman.

The lessons presented here are kept short intentionally. I have experienced God in simple, common-sense, practical ways, and I believe that is the best way for me to communicate His word. Remember, each of us experiences God in a unique way, and we can best communicate that unique perspective of His character in the way it is revealed to us.

I believe the reason God has called me to write this book is because the lessons given to me over the years were never intended for just me or my local Sunday school classes. I have observed the need within the church for us all to experience God personally in practical ways. God wants to be involved in our everyday, moment-by-moment experiences. Our faith should influence our behavior at work on Monday in the same way it does at church on Sunday.

Also, it is important for all of us inside the church to understand the awesome responsibility we have to those outside the church looking in. Statistically, on any given Sunday, around 70 percent of the local community is not in church. What message are we sending? Is it practical? Does it make good common sense? Does it meet people at the level of their need? Is it attractive? Are we prepared if someone walks in from the outside? These are hard questions for the church to answer, but we are the church, and we hold the ultimate responsibility for sharing God's love with the world. The purpose of Christian education is "to prepare God's people" (Ephesians 4:12-13) to be responsible for the answers to questions such as these.

I have a few suggestions regarding how to read and use the lessons in this book. Each lesson is developed around a central theme or focus point presented at the beginning of each lesson along with the foundational scripture. I suggest that you think about the focus point and read the foundational scripture from your Bible before going to the lesson. The various insights from the lesson will have more meaning and will stimulate your thinking, which is the ultimate purpose of all the lessons. They are designed to cause you to think about your daily connection with God.

I recommend that you set aside one week for each lesson. Read the foundational scripture and the lesson on the first day. At the end of each lesson is an application and action section. There are five activities in each section; complete one activity each day for five days.

If you speed through the lessons in a quick read, you will speed right past the deep thinking and personal application the lessons may hold for you. While some of the lessons may hold answers and insight, that is not the primary intent. The lessons are designed to cause you to think about your life, your personal relationship with God, and your own lessons for a lifetime. Be sure to keep a journal, so you may record your spiritual insights and thoughts as you read each lesson.

If you are a teacher using these lessons with an adult Sunday school class or Bible study, use each lesson and application and action activity as a general reading and activity guideline for the week prior to the formal class meeting. Try adding your own personal examples during the class meeting to emphasize the spiritual insights from the lesson, along with discussion central to the theme of the application and action section. For a detailed leader's guide, see the appendix.

If you are an individual reader, this is not a chance encounter or random event. I believe God asked me to write this book for you and has ordained your appointment with me and this book. Use it as your daily devotional guide, following the instructions above regarding setting aside one week for each lesson. I pray that this book will be something specific for you and meet you at the level of your spiritual need.

I try to avoid too much personal opinion, but you will find my opinions in some of these lessons. None are intended to be controversial, and I have prayed over them many times. Keep an open mind and understand that differing opinions will never change the simple message of God's love, forgiveness, and grace.

Yes, this book serves as a marker of another small start in my life. Only God knows its full intent, but I would be honored for small groups to use this book in their Bible studies, seeking believers to use this book in their daily devotions, and searching Sunday school teachers to use this book as a guide for their lessons. However, I believe there is a spiritual intent beyond my vision, and I pray that my effort to yet another small start in my life may speak to you about a God of love and everlasting hope whose greatest desire is a personal relationship with you.

David Byrd
Spring 2005

Lesson One:
Driving in the Fog

Focus Point:

God uses adversity to teach us
important lessons.

Foundational Scripture:

O Lord, open his eyes so he may see.

2 Kings 6:17

Driving in the Fog

*H*ave you ever had to drive through a heavy fog? I am talking about the kind of fog that is so thick you can only see the front of your car.

In the predawn hours of a December morning a few years ago, I was driving to a friend's ranch just south of my home town. I had made this trip many times, but this time was different. There was a heavy fog.

My friend's ranch is located in a river bottom, and as I got closer to the river, the fog had slowed me to a crawl. I was confident that I could find the turn which led to my friend's drive because the location was so familiar. But no matter how slow the pace or how close to the side of the road I drove, I could not find the turn. Nothing looked the same.

Finally, out of desperation, I pulled over to the shoulder of the road, stopped, and turned off the ignition. I reasoned that I was close to the turn and would wait for the sun to come up. With some light, I could easily find my way.

As I sat by the roadside, I began to see things that I had never noticed before. My vision was limited to those things nearby. The fog was blocking my long-range vision, so those things immediately near were in vivid focus. I was surprised by a fox stalking a rabbit, and then a few minutes later I saw a bobcat walk by the car in hot pursuit of them both. I saw things that morning that I would have never seen had the fog not slowed me to a stop. When the morning sun finally burned off enough of the fog to light my way, I was surprised to find that I was almost a mile away from the turn. I thought I was so close. Had I not stopped and waited for the sun's light, I would have been even farther from my destination.

It was several days later before I recognized that God had used that foggy December morning to teach me a great lesson about life. Adversity is much like fog in our lives, and sometimes God will use the fog of adversity to teach and direct us. Just like driving in the fog, adversity slows us to a crawl and sometimes brings us to a complete stop. It limits our long-range vision, making it difficult for us to find our way. When facing adversity, our attention is often focused on those things that we may not see at the normal pace of life, possibly those things that matter most.

Adversity and, especially, tragedy are a part of life, and I find it difficult to believe that our loving heavenly Father sends it to hurt us. But I can confirm, from personal experience, that He uses all things and pulls them together for the good of His children (Romans 8:28). It makes sense that God would use the occasions of adversity in our lives to teach us necessary life lessons.

If you think about it, most of our significant lessons are stimulated by adversity. There is no better classroom in which to learn important life lessons than Adversity 101.

The Bible is filled with stories of people being guided through adversity by a loving God. One of my favorite stories is about Elisha, the intern of the great Elijah (2 Kings Chapter 2). The Bible records that Elijah was taken by a chariot of fire directly to heaven.

When Elijah departed, God blessed his intern, Elisha, with a double portion of power, and in his lifetime Elisha performed almost two times the number of miracles as Elijah. Other than Moses, he was the only person in the Old Testament to perform more miracles than Elijah.

One of Elisha's miracles recorded in the Bible is an occasion when Elisha and his servant were surrounded by the Aramean army (2 Kings 6:8-22). The army was determined to kill Elisha and his servant. The servant was in a state of great fear and could not understand why Elisha was so confident.

Elisha prayed and asked God to open the eyes of his servant that he may see their spiritual protection. Immediately, the servant's spiritual eyes were opened, and he saw thousands of angels surrounding the Aramean army, protecting him and Elisha. The servant quickly understood why Elisha's calm, trusting demeanor was of merit. He saw and thus understood that their spiritual protection was greater than those who were physically threatening them.

Do you think the servant could have effectively learned this profound lesson of trusting faith from some seminar taught under the comfort of a shade tree? No. A lesson this significant required the classroom of adversity.

Another example of a lesson learned in adversity is the story of the conversion of Saul of Tarsus found in Acts Chapter 9. Saul was a determined persecutor of the grass-root Christian community. He was met on the road to Damascus by a vision of light. Those who were with him heard a great noise, but Saul heard a voice saying, "Saul, why do you persecute me?" Saul replied, "Who are you, Lord?" "I am Jesus," the voice answered. When Saul recovered from his vision, he was blinded by the great light. He was slowed to a crawl, totally dependent on those around him for guidance. Later we find that God was using this time of Saul's disability to have him in deep thought about what he had heard and about his future direction. Saul became the apostle Paul and served God's purpose as the bridge for all Gentiles to the Christian faith. In addition, he wrote most of the New Testament.

Do you think Paul would have decided on this new direction in his life had he not encountered the adversity of the blinding light? I do not think so.

From my personal experience on that foggy December morning, I have learned three things. First, even though God may not intentionally send the fog of adversity or tragedy, He uses that time to teach and direct us. The fog of adversity slows our pace from the hustle and bustle of life. Our vision is limited to the immediate, and God can show us things of significance. We can focus on what matters most.

Second, God has our attention in the fog of adversity. God's greatest desire is a personal relationship with each of us. However, our attention is often distracted, and we become preoccupied with the world around us. But in the fog of adversity, our attention is vividly focused on a source of light to show us the way. Our attention is a commodity which should always be invested wisely.

Third, when it comes to our spiritual best interest, fog is good, not bad. We are conditioned to think that anything slowing us down or bringing us to a stop is bad – not so at the spiritual level. The next time you face adversity, look for what God may show you. After the lesson learned from my experience in the fog, I now see adversity as an opportunity to learn and possibly redirect my attention.

When you are faced with your own personal fog, ask God to show you what He wants you to see and where He wants you to go. Remember, God is able to work all things together for good for those who love Him and are called to His purpose (Romans 8:28).

Application and Action

Day One: As you go through your normal routine today, intentionally slow down an activity that you normally speed through. It could be as simple as slowly pulling into your parking space at work; just intentionally slow down one activity.

Day Two: If you decided to intentionally slow the pace of some specific area of your life, what things of significance would you notice or act on that are being ignored at your current pace?

Day Three: What is the most important lesson you have learned from adversity? Why is adversity such a great teacher? How will the answer to this question benefit you in your life's journey?

Day Four: Our attention is a commodity which should be invested wisely. What are your top three attention priorities? Are you satisfied with your list? If not, how will you change it?

Day Five: God speaks to each of us. Be sure to keep a journal. Write a brief summary of your spiritual insights and thoughts from this week's lesson.

Lesson Two:
Doin' What's Right

Focus Point:

The act of doing what is morally
right releases spiritual power that extends
beyond our human understanding.

Scriptural Foundation:

*In everything, do to others what you
would have them do to you.*

Matthew 7:12

Doin' What's Right

Our lives are notched with significant events, some happy, some sad. The passing of my parents was probably one of the most significant life events for me. My dad crossed over to heaven's side in August 1991 and my mother in November 2003. God chose the setting of my mother's funeral for one of my lifetime lessons.

My mother died at age ninety-six. She had outlived or distanced most of her nephews, so our family was having difficulty finding pall bearers physically able to perform. My brother, Gary, who still lives near our home town in South Carolina, gave me a call prior to my trip back home for the funeral, and we were discussing this issue. I suggested our old home church and some of the people who would remember my mother. One person specifically came to mind: Al Putnam. Al and I graduated from high school together, and during our teen years, we had been very active in the church youth program. My mother had been one of the leaders of that program as far back as I can remember. I knew if Al was still there, he would be happy to help.

Mother's funeral was a touching event. People who remembered her from our old home church came to support and help. I also noticed that my friend Al was there serving as a pall bearer. After the graveside service, Al came up to me, and we reconnected after some twenty-five years. The members of our home church had asked the family to come back for coffee at the church, and Al asked if I would join them.

Back in the church meeting center, Al came over and sat down beside me. We discussed old times and memories between welcomed interruptions of well wishers. When it came time to leave, I stood and turned to Al to say goodbye. He looked at me as if he had something on his mind that had gone unsaid and asked if we could speak privately. "Of course," I said, and we went into a back room and closed the door. What happened then will forever change the way I think of my fellow man and the spiritual importance of, as we say in the deep south, "doin' what's right."

My friend Al reminded me of a time years earlier when I was the owner of a construction company in my home town. He said, "Twenty-five years ago you did some work on my house." I hesitated for a moment because I thought Al was preparing me for some twenty-five-year-old warranty work. But that was not the direction of this conversation. With a sense of resolve in his eyes, he said, "You never invoiced me, and I owe you $900. It has bothered me for a long time, and when you asked me to participate in your mother's funeral, I knew it was my opportunity to do the right thing. I always pay my bills!"

Now, Al was being a little too hard on himself because, for some reason, I never knew that he owed this money. I had moved to Texas many years prior, and we had lost touch. In fact, I would have preferred that we just forget the whole thing. I acknowledged Al's fine sense of integrity and asked him to keep his money. This is where this special story gets interesting.

Bear with me as I leave, for a moment, the story of Al and tell you about my prayer the night before. My wife, Mary, and I had been praying for a very special person in our lives who was going through some difficult times. Even though this person had never asked us for financial assistance, we both felt that we should help in some way. We knew that this person had an immediate short-term need of $450, so we asked God to show us how He wanted us to help. After praying, a scripture verse just popped into my mind; it was the verse where God promises that He is able to do far more than we can ask or imagine (Ephesians 3:20).

Go with me now back to my friend Al. In private, he had handed me an envelope with nine, one hundred dollar bills in it. When the envelope touched my hand, it did not feel like my money. I asked Al to take the money back, but as he leaned away, he said, "I can't take it back because I'll lose the blessing for doin' what's right."

At that time I had not yet connected all the dots. I expressed to Al how uncomfortable I felt about taking the money, and to that he said, "If you feel that way, why don't you do something special with it...like help someone!" Sometimes God has to use a sledge hammer to get my attention! The reality of what was happening hit me. God had answered my prayer for our special friend by providing exactly two times the immediate financial need (far more than we asked or imagined). Additionally, He had blessed an old friend for doin' what's right, and He had used the special setting of my mother's funeral for a miracle to teach me that I should be ever watchful for answered prayer because, sometimes, it comes in unmarked packages.

The Bible speaks of doin' what's right in Psalms Chapter 15. Verse four says that a Godly person honors his word even when it hurts. It was the beginning of the Christmas season, and I am sure Al could have used that money for his family. But Al made a decision to do what God had told him to do – the right thing. Al's actions set in motion a series of miraculous events that immediately blessed many people, and those blessings continue.

For example, that evening I had the privilege and blessing of having my entire family witness the presentation of this special God-directed gift to our dear friend. They all heard the story of the "miracle money."

The act of doing the morally right thing releases spiritual power that extends beyond our human understanding. Only God knows the full impact of this story of Al's simple act of doin' what's right.

I believe God honors the lives of people who do the right things for the right reasons. Normally, we all have this internal code that alerts us to right and wrong. However, our responses to the circumstances of our daily lives condition that internal code. Some begin to justify their actions based on a balance system that always seems to favor their own special interest. Some justify actions based on whether or not they will get caught or be exposed. Some determine their actions based on what they feel is right, no matter what the outcome. Psalms 15 refers to the latter as the righteous ones who will live on God's holy hill.

In most circumstances, right or wrong can be justified or argued either way. But every time we justify our actions as right, when deep down we know they are wrong, we condition that internal code to not make us feel so bad the next time. When we make a habit of justifying the "rightness" of all our actions over a lifetime, we become numb to our God-given internal code of right and wrong.

I have known very few people who had the integrity to do the right thing even when it hurt. I have, at times in my past, fallen short of that standard myself. But God calls us to live above our human instincts and reactions. The standard called for in Psalms Chapter 15 is a spiritual standard of honor. None of us can understand it from a worldly perspective; it can only be spiritually discerned.

What is the answer for us Christians who have been called to do the right thing even when it hurts? The question is universal, but the answer is personal. I cannot answer this for anyone other than myself.

The life lesson from my friend Al is worth far more than $900. I have personally witnessed the power of doin' what's right. So, my personal answer is to apply this standard of honor to every area of my life – no matter what!

Application and Action

Day One: Read Psalms Chapter 15. How do you personally interpret this chapter? How does this scripture apply to you? Why?

Day Two: Read Ephesians 3:20. How is this verse related to Psalms 15:4? How does this understanding specifically relate to you?

Day Three: How can something make sense spiritually but not make sense from a worldly perspective? Why is it important for you to understand this?

Day Four: Write your own definition of spiritual power.

Day Five: God speaks to each of us. Be sure to keep a journal. Write a brief summary of your spiritual insights and thoughts from this week's lesson.

Lesson Three:
The Day of Small Things

Focus Point:

The smallest beginnings are better
than the greatest intentions.

Scriptural Foundation:

Who despises the day of small things?

Zechariah 4:10

The Day of Small Things

*B*oth my daughters, Lauren and Jenni, are mature, successful women today with families of their own. But forever etched in my memory are their first steps. Those unsure, awkward, and often meandering first steps have matured over the years into confident strides of adulthood. Their focus now is on their individual, daily walk – their life's journey. I am sure they give little thought to those first steps, and so it is with all of us.

We tend to reduce the importance of our small starts to a level of insignificance. As a result, we sometimes fail to act on possible life-changing opportunities and growth. Often, beginnings seem like a waste of time in comparison to the mountain of work needed to realize a vision or complete a goal. But it is those beginnings, those small starts, which set in motion the ultimate impact of our lives. Most of our personal achievement and growth is driven by seemingly insignificant beginnings or first steps.

I began teaching an adult Sunday school class many years ago with the intention of doing it for only six months. I never considered that God would call me to a life's work and purpose from that small first step. In fact, if God had told me His plan, I may have never begun. I was unsure, uncertain, insecure, and scared. But from that small start, God has called me to a life's work. From this work I have witnessed miracles, seen lives changed, and watched as new teachers were encouraged to go and do the same. God has a way of generating significant impact from seemingly insignificant events.

The prophet Zechariah delivered a similar message from God to Zerubbabel, governor of Judah, in approximately 520 B.C.E. Zerubbabel had been chosen by God to rebuild the temple which had been destroyed by the Babylonians in approximately 586 B.C.E.

According to the book of Zechariah, the task given Zerubbabel seemed so overwhelming that after he laid the foundation, he began to procrastinate. In fact, he put it off for eighteen years. God's people were going about their own business, building their own homes, but God's work of rebuilding the temple was being put off to another day (Haggai 1:2,4-6,9). The people of Judah had great intentions. I am sure they discussed it at their Sabbath meetings and talked about what great things they would do – someday. That is, until Zechariah showed up with a simple, history-changing message from God.

Zechariah was a prophet contemporary to this particular time. His prophesies encouraged God's people and were usually consistent in theme. But this message was different. It was so simple that most people who heard it probably missed it – so simple that it was confusing!

Have you ever heard something that seemed so simple that your first response was, "It can't be that easy"? Zechariah's message from God to the leader Zerubbabel was like that. God said, "Who despises the day of small things?" (Zechariah 4:10).

It was as if Zechariah was reading Zerubbabel's mind. God's mission seemed so overpowering to Zerubbabel that he had overlooked the simple task of starting. Many times he had thought about starting, and many times he had grand intentions of starting, but the overwhelming big picture got in the way. *How can we do this? What about that? What about lumber? We'll have to float the logs by sea. Did you say float the logs for the lumber?* I can imagine the discussions. I have witnessed planning meetings like that, where everything is discussed – except getting started.

The great basketball coach John Wooden had a teaching point that he used over the years with members of his teams: "Never let what you can't do get in the way of what you can do." Start with your strengths, and do what you can. It sounds too simple, but that philosophy produced some of the all-time basketball greats.

God's message to Zerubbabel was to appreciate the significance of the small act of starting, and leave the big picture to Him. These instructions from God required more than just good intentions. In essence, God was saying, *Focus on what you can do, and trust Me with what you cannot do.*

I vividly remember the day my dad announced to the family that he had been laid off by the textile company that had employed him for over thirty-five years. I was twelve years old and did not fully understand the ramifications of this announcement. Dad was fifty-six; he had one son in college, a family, two weeks severance, and no hopes for another job. He looked at my mother and asked, "Lillie, what are we going to do?" She replied, "God will make a way."

They discussed many options that evening, and as I listened with as much adult interest as I could muster, daddy told mama that he had always wanted to build a store in our front yard. We had a big front yard, and we lived on a busy highway that connected our home town with a local lake where thousands of people visited each year to fish and vacation. Mama said, "Let's do it," but daddy was reluctant to get started because, as he put it, "We don't know how to run a store." I will never forget my mother's next words: "And we'll never know until we start."

Daddy and mama opened that store within six months. They built it into a profitable venture that supported the family for thirteen years and sent two sons through college and graduate school. They focused on what they could do and trusted God for all the things they could not do.

Zerubbabel had allowed what he thought he could not do to get in the way of what he could do; therefore, God made the message even more outrageous. He asked, "Who despises the day of small things?" Then He added, "Men will rejoice when they see the plumb line in the hand of Zerubbabel" (Zechariah 4:10). The plumb line was a basic string with a weight on one end, and it was used to make construction walls level and straight. God was encouraging the governor to just pick up the plumb line. I am sure that sounded too simple to Zerubbabel. He probably thought, *It can't be that easy.*

History tells us the temple was completed four years from the day the governor decided to act on that encouraging word from God and just pick up a string. As unbelievable as it may seem, the simple act of picking up a string was the stimulus which began the significant driving force among God's people for a great project and accomplishment. The smallest beginnings are better than the greatest intentions.

We are all God's children on this earthly walk, and opportunity knocks for everyone, but we are conditioned to allow the size of the opportunity to discourage us from ever beginning. This story of God's word to a reluctant and procrastinating Jewish governor encourages us to always act on what we can do and trust God with what we cannot do.

Application and Action

Day One: Think of a significant accomplishment in your life. What was your first step or action taken toward that accomplishment? Write a brief description of how you felt about that small step at the time.

Day Two: Small steps seem so insignificant, but great accomplishments always have small beginnings. Also, God sees us in a future that He has planned and as we can be rather than as we are. Read Jeremiah 29:11. How does this spiritual understanding relate to you?

Day Three: Everyone has unique talents and abilities. What are yours? List your strengths, talents, and abilities. Focus on those which are very unique to you.

Day Four: Think of one situation in which you allowed the big picture to keep you from beginning.

How has this lesson caused you to think differently about beginnings?

Day Five: God speaks to each of us. Be sure to keep a journal. Write a brief summary of your spiritual insights and thoughts from this week's lesson.

Lesson Four:
Higher Ground

Focus Point:

God calls us to live above

our circumstances, not in them.

Scriptural Foundation:

And a highway will be there.

Isaiah 35:8-9

Higher Ground

One of the most amazing things about God and His creation is the uniqueness of each individual. Each of us was created to grasp and understand a special part of God's character. In other words, each of us experiences God in a unique way. Some see and experience God in deep theological understanding, while others feel God's presence in worship and song. We individually experience Him differently. Yes, I do understand that God never changes (Malachi 3:6), but He has designed a unique and diverse creation that experiences Him in many different ways.

Over the years I have had several Christian friends and role models who have shared a wealth of insight with me about how they experience God. In casual conversation, I always encourage them to describe their personal experiences with God. In almost every example, I hear uniqueness in their individual experiences. One describes how God speaks directly to him, while another explains an inner sense of

God's will for her life – same God, different experience.

I have experienced God in very practical, common, even simple ways. I feel blessed with the opportunity of experiencing Him in everyday, common events. For example, I heard a song recently with lyrics so spiritually insightful that it was as if God was speaking directly to me. Now the artist was singing the lyrics from a secular perspective, but that did not interfere with God's message – a message about higher ground.

The Old Testament references high ground as a good place to be. It was even considered holy ground when Moses received the Ten Commandments on Mount Sinai. Three disciples, James, John, and Peter, were on a mountain when they witnessed the spiritual transfiguration of Jesus and saw Him walking and talking with Moses and Elijah (Mark 9:2-4).

Jesus preached a great sermon from higher ground (Matthew 5:1). In that famous Sermon on the Mount (Matthew Chapter 5, 6, and 7), He laid the foundation for His short ministry here on earth and for His eternal message to us. His simple message is this: God loves each of us, and the most important issue in our life is our connection with Him. Why? Because when we have that connection, we can trust Him to guide and care for us. Without that connection it is just us on our own with more uncontrollable circumstances than we can shake a stick at.

In that same sermon, Jesus said not to worry about the circumstances of life, for worry is a waste of time (Matthew 6:25-27). This was radical thinking for that generation, and it still is today.

I just received an email prayer request for the family of a young man sixteen years of age who was found dead in his bed this morning. I have friends fighting cancer, getting fired, closing businesses, going broke, and experiencing broken homes – too much for anyone to handle alone. However, Jesus said, "In this world you will have trouble. But take heart! I have overcome the world" (John 16:33).

Okay, that sounds good, but what do we do with the overwhelming curve balls that life can throw our way? We must climb to higher ground, for God calls us to live above our circumstances, not in them.

Imagine you are on the longest and hardest walk of your life. In fact, the walk *is* your life. Just the walk itself would be difficult, but your walk is extra hard because you have a big bag to drag with you. What bag? Look at it; it has a large sign on the side with red letters that read, *My Circumstances.*

You have tried to tend it, delegate it, ignore it, lose it, and run from it, but none of that works. Every turn you take leads you back to that big bag. The bad part is… it is bigger now than it was the last time you looked at it!

You look around at others on the same walk and see some with bags smaller than yours and some larger. But that is no consolation because all you have time for is your own bag.

While you are struggling with the debilitating weight of your bag, trying to keep pace with the walk, you hear a small voice behind you saying, *Why don't you join Me up here?* You look up and sense that God is calling you. He is. He is calling you to higher ground.

The encouragement of His voice makes you feel better, and a feeling of genuine thankfulness floods your soul, just to know that your Creator really cares. However, those feelings quickly dissipate when your attention shifts back to your circumstances – your big bag.

How can you answer God's call and climb this spiritual mountain with a heavy, burdensome bag? You cannot! The only way for you to heed God's call to higher ground is to leave that big bag at the foot of the hill. God wants you to live above your circumstances, not in them.

Living on higher ground does not isolate us from our circumstances or make them go away. In fact, we can still see them at the bottom of the hill. The difference is that we can trust God to keep up with our big bag because God is able to work all things together for the good of those who love Him and are called according to His purpose (Romans 8:28).

On higher ground we can see clearly with spiritual eyes (2 Corinthians 5:7), and we can think clearly with the help of the Holy Spirit (John 14:26). This radical lifestyle looks foolish to the world (John 14:17), but life is abundant (John 10:10) on higher ground. The next time you feel it necessary to complain about your human plight, remember, God is always calling you to higher ground.

Application and Action

Day One: How does this lesson about higher ground apply to you personally?

Day Two: Your life should never be defined by your circumstances. What is the meaning of this statement for you personally?

Day Three: Read Matthew 6:33-34. One of the requirements of climbing to spiritually higher ground is to give up – not quit, but give up dragging your big bag. Name one issue of personal worry that you can give up to God.

Day Four: Another requirement of living on spiritual higher ground is trust. We start with faith, which is a conscious act of our wills, and as God proves Himself (Psalms 34:8), our faith matures into a level of trust. On a scale of one to ten (one being the lowest and ten being the highest), rank your spiritual trust level. What steps of faith can you act on that will move you to the next level?

Day Five: God speaks to each of us. Be sure to keep a journal. Write a brief summary of your spiritual insights and thoughts from this week's lesson.

Lesson Five:
Crossing Jordan

Focus Point:

God's power is released on earth
when we act on our faith.

Scriptural Foundation:

See, I have given you this land.

Deuteronomy 1:8

Crossing Jordan

The Bible comes to life when we experience its validity on a personal level. Some debate the historical, scientific, or literary validity of the Bible, but it seems that those debates pale in significance to the message the Bible holds for each of us individually.

For example, recently I was reading through the book of Deuteronomy and verse eight in the first chapter caught my attention. This is where Moses confirms what God had promised a generation before to the children of Israel. Moses told them that God had said, "I have given you this land" – the Promised Land. Not if, not maybe, not some day, but "I have."

God's promise to the Israelites was emphatic: The land is yours! Yet, as they camped out on the side of the Jordan River, doubt and fear took control of their emotions. The twelve spies that had crossed over Jordan to scout out the Promised Land reported that they saw "giants" and "great walls" (Deuteronomy

1:28). All but Caleb and Joshua said takeover was impossible, and the mission should be forgotten. The chatter among the people went something like this: *Let's walk around the desert some more, or maybe we could go back to Egypt; slavery wasn't so bad!* Fear of the unknown can lead us to some crazy decisions.

The decision was made, against the pleadings of Moses, to walk around the desert some more. In fact, God let them walk around the desert long enough for that entire generation to pass away before He led them back to the Jordan River. What a lost opportunity. An entire generation said no to the promise of God. Why? Doubt and fear.

As I read this story, I asked myself, *How many of God's promises have I turned my back on because of doubt and fear?* Valid questions for all of us are these: *Am I camped out on the side of **my** Jordan River? Am I intending to cross the river, maybe playing church or talking about God, but really too afraid to get my feet wet?* There is a great lesson in this story: The generation of Israelites who missed the Promised Land missed it because they refused to claim the power of God's promise.

Years later God led a new generation of Israelites back to the Jordan River, but this time was different. This generation of God's chosen had a faith that had matured to a level of trust. God had also raised a great leader in Joshua. When Joshua instructed the priests to carry the Ark of the Covenant across the Jordan River, which happened to be at flood stage, there was no hesitancy. The priests stepped into the swift and swollen Jordan on faith, and the river stopped flowing and stacked up on the upstream side while the future nation of Israel crossed over to the Promised Land (Joshua 3:15-17). God's promise was finally claimed by a trusting people.

This is a wonderful story of God's promise and provision, but it is more than just a nice old history lesson. In its deeper meaning, God provides spiritual insight into our lives today through three direct parallels.

First, like the Israelites in the desert on a journey to who knows where with no visible provisions, we are born into an insecure world and spend the rest of our earthly existence desperately seeking security. I have friends who have spent the majority of their lives searching for that much needed sense of security. They reason that maybe a new love, a new friend, a new place, a new car, or more money will bring them security. We all sometimes get lost in this worldly journey looking for some "thing" to make us feel secure.

The Israelites were no different. They got lost and they complained, so God personally guided them (Exodus 13:21). They needed water and they complained, so God made the bitter water sweet (Exodus 15:24-25). They were hungry and they complained, so God provided quail and a bread-like substance called manna (Exodus 16:8). Oh, by the way, God promised them manna every morning and told them not to store it but to gather only what they needed for that day, trusting Him for tomorrow, but they stored it anyway, and it spoiled over night (Exodus 16:20).

The Israelites' futile search for security is a familiar example. The children of Israel looked for security in the things that God could provide, rather than in the source of it all – God Himself! Does this sound familiar?

Second, the Jordan was crossed on faith. There was no bridge, no life jackets, and no visible means of assistance. Also, the Jordan was at flood stage. Most of us would suggest waiting for a better time when crossing might not be quite so difficult. This concept of crossing Jordan on faith parallels the personal, spiritual decision we all must make. We connect with God by faith, and the power of His promises is released when we exercise (act on) that faith.

That personal, spiritual decision is our Jordan. If we refuse to act on that decision by faith, we continue to wander in the desert. God is still there, He still loves us, and His greatest desire is to connect with us, but He cannot help us because we have refused to exercise our faith and accept His promises of love, forgiveness, and grace.

What is faith? The Bible describes it as "being sure of what we hope for and certain of what we do not see" (Hebrews 11:1). That sounds foolish to our human understanding, but faith is something that must be understood spiritually because it makes no sense from a worldly or intellectual perspective. The trusting generation of Israelites exercised their faith and stepped into the flooding Jordan. That act made no sense intellectually, but it was perfectly clear to Joshua and the children of Israel through the spiritual eyes of their trusting faith.

The third parallel is the best. Remember the first generation of wandering Israelites who failed to exercise their faith and turned their back on God's promise? God's promise had no power for them, though it would for the next generation – same God, same promise, different result. Why? The first generation of Israelites under the leadership of Moses recognized God for His daily provisions but chose not to trust Him for tomorrow. They failed to learn their most important lesson: God's power is released on earth when we act on our faith today and trust God's promise for tomorrow.

Yes, all of us are on our own personal journey. On this journey we are faced with choices, just like the Israelites. We can choose to act on faith and experience God's power and provision, or we can decide to trust in our own human understanding. Our human nature and society lead us to believe that material things represent security and are the most important issues of life. However, the story of the wandering Israelites tells us that the spiritual decisions we make are far more important, and only through a connection with God can we find the answers to our desperate search for security. Like the children of Israel learned, the ultimate security is to rest in the power of God's love by faith (Matthew 7:24-25).

Application and Action

Day One: What will be the ultimate, most significant decision of your life? Why?

Day Two: What role does faith play in your connection with God?

Day Three: God's power is released on earth through the exercise of our faith (Matthew 17:20). How does this scripture relate to your current concept of faith?

Day Four: Faith requires actions rather than intentions. Read James 2:17. How is this understanding important to you? How can you put your faith into action?

Day Five: God speaks to each of us. Be sure to keep a journal. Write a brief summary of your spiritual insights and thoughts from this week's lesson.

Lesson Six: Convenient Confusion

Focus Point:

God never wants us to be confused about who He is or our personal relationship with Him.

Scriptural Foundation:

We have not received the spirit of the world but the Spirit who is from God, that we may understand what God has freely given us.

I Corinthians 2:12

Convenient Confusion

Why did God make life so complicated?
I gave up on God when I was a teenager because I had a bad
experience with church.
How can a good God allow bad things to happen?

I have personally heard these statements and
questions from people who claimed to be
spiritually confused. The confusion was real but also
very convenient. Their convenient confusion was
seemingly a rational excuse to hide from God.

Life can be confusing at times, and there will
always be questions to which there seem to be no easy
answers. But when we choose to remain lost in our
confusion, we hide from God and miss the ultimate
meaning of life.

I am an archery enthusiast. It is a great hobby, and
at one time I traveled the state in competitive events.
Through this hobby I developed a friendship with a
person who is an excellent archer. I learned a lot from
him, and we traveled to many archery tournaments
together. I did not know exactly where my friend

stood on spiritual issues. I knew he was not a member of a church nor did he attend church, so one Saturday afternoon on a long drive back home from a tournament, I found the opportunity to bring up the subject of his position on certain important spiritual issues.

I started by asking my friend if he ever attended church. He responded with a short "No." My follow up question was this: "Have you ever considered the importance of your relationship with God?" His response to that question brings us to the very point of this lesson.

He said, "O yes, I believe in God, but when I was a teenager I had a bad experience with church. I decided if that is what church is all about, I don't want to have any more to do with it." The story goes on, and I can say that some progress was made, but the point is my friend had used this confusion from his teenage years as a convenient excuse to hide from God for the rest of his life.

From years of experience, I have found that this is not an isolated case. Many people use spiritual confusion as a convenient excuse to hide from God. They reason that it would be impossible to consider God in their life because they are confused and do not have the answers to all their spiritual questions. To the confused it sounds reasonable and logical, but not from God's perspective. God never wants us to be confused about who He is or the importance of our relationship with Him.

I have another friend who has wrestled with his intellectual understanding of the Bible for over twenty years. He reasons that he cannot deal with God on a personal level until he has all the logical answers to all his spiritual questions. This response to life from a position of spiritual confusion seems very logical to him, but not to God.

Now some may take me to task on this issue and say that I am being too hard with those who claim spiritual confusion as a reason to deny their connection with God. Some may also say that I should be more compassionate and understanding. I agree that spiritual confusion is a real issue for many people, and I will always agree to err on the side of compassion. But I will never sit by and watch someone miss a personal relationship with our Creator by simply accepting his or her confusion as an excuse – especially when there is a very simple answer to that confusion.

The simple answer to all spiritual confusion is this: BECOME A SEEKER!

As an agnostic, C. S. Lewis started on a mission to systematically prove what he saw as the obvious contradictions in the Bible. To support his claims, he decided to become an unbiased critic. To do so he had to become a seeker of spiritual truth. Through his search of the Bible, he found the core issue to which there is no contradiction: God's unconditional love for all mankind. Rather than drawing the conclusion that the Bible is too confusing, he became a seeker of truth. Little did he know that there are undeniable promises from God which tell us those who seek will find (Matthew 7:7).

With the intent of critical review, C. S. Lewis met God on a personal level and became one of the most prolific Christian writers of all time. I am sure C. S.

Lewis never had all the spiritual answers, but he chose not to remain in his intellectual confusion. He found God simply by deciding to spiritually seek Him.

Some of the most sincere, life-changing stories begin with the prayer, *God if you're out there, I really want to know you.* Contrast that with this statement: *I will ignore the implications of God in my life until I have deeper intellectual understanding and answers to all my questions. I am not responsible; I am confused.* Therein stands the difference between spiritual seekers and the spiritually confused.

I must admit, there have been times in my life when the convenience of confusion seemed more comfortable than seeking. But I can personally endorse the life-changing process of being a seeker. I do not have the answers to all my spiritual questions, but I have found God and no longer hide behind confusion – no matter how convenient.

Application and Action

Day One: Have you ever been spiritually confused? Compile a list of your questions and issues about which you are spiritually confused.

Day Two: Look at your list from Day One. Have any of these unanswered questions or issues of confusion ever come between you and God? Write a few sentences describing your feelings about your list.

Day Three: Read Jeremiah 29:11-13 and Matthew 7:7-8. How does the spiritual understanding of these two scriptures apply to your list from Day One?

Day Four: How can you personally become a better seeker? Read Luke 18:16-17. Can you entrust your questions and confusion to God, believing that He will provide understanding later? How?

Day Five: God speaks to each of us. Be sure to keep a journal. Write a brief summary of your spiritual insights and thoughts from this week's lesson.

Lesson Seven:
A Heart of Wisdom

Focus Point:

The demonstration of God's love
comes from a heart of wisdom.

Scriptural Foundation:

*Teach us to number our days aright,
that we may gain a heart of wisdom.*

Psalms 90:12

A Heart of Wisdom

We are each accountable for how we portray God's love to the world. We can never expect the world to change until we are willing to become the change that is needed in the world – accountability begins with you and me.

As part of the contemporary Christian community, I observe two differing groups. The first group I identify as the intellectual or knowledge-based Christians. Characteristic of this group is the context of their logic which includes the perception of having all the answers, knowing all the rules, and the insistence on debating spiritual issues. The problem is the answers are sometimes complex, the rules change between denominations, and intellectual debate never seems to confirm spiritual truth.

I like to call the second group the heart of wisdom Christians. They seem to be in touch with their imperfection, realistic about life's answers, and they see a distinguishing difference between intellectual knowledge and spiritual truth. Characteristic of this group is the way they demonstrate God's love with their lives and the way they deal with others.

Now, intellectual head knowledge from Bible study is important in understanding our relationship with God, and I would never criticize the intellectual foundation of our spiritual Christian leaders. However, if that intellectual understanding never makes the transforming journey from the head to the heart, we tend to become judgmental and sometimes distort the real, true message of God's love.

Have you ever been challenged by a Christian friend or group to take a stand for or support some cause that you were not quite sure about? Usually it is presented that a simple yes or no will put you on the "right" side of the issue. But you must choose one of two lines. One line puts you on the popular or presumptuous right side. The other line is not only considered the wrong side but may be misconstrued as condoning the wrong. You may not feel in your heart that either line is exclusively right or wrong, but you feel pressured to be in the right line. If you should choose the wrong line or abstain from either line, you may not be seen as a good person or as an acceptable Christian. Well, join the club. You and I may be the only members, but I have been in that very situation plenty of times.

Jesus was faced with a similar scenario with a woman who had been caught in the very act of adultery (John 8:3-11). The woman was thrown to the ground at Jesus' feet by a group of religious leaders and a belligerent crowd of followers. One of the leaders explained to Jesus, "This woman has been caught in the very act of adultery, and the Law says we should stone her to death. What do you say?"

What a tough question! If Jesus said yes, he would have been in agreement with the Law, but he also would have condemned the woman to death on the spot. Many of the people involved with this crowd were probably thinking, *If Jesus will just get in line with the religious leaders, he will be accepted as a righteous member of the group, but if he says this woman should not be stoned, he will be condoning her sin.*

The self-assuming godly people and religious experts were telling Jesus to get in one line or the other.

Jesus used this opportunity to demonstrate the uniqueness of God's love and to challenge us to look at our own sin first. He said, "He who is without sin may cast the first stone." I love this story because it provides me with a simple solution to those difficult questions for which there are no simple answers. The simple solution is this: We must place priority on love before judgment. Jesus' message to the intellectual experts was clear – their priorities were backwards.

We must be discerning about all issues, and spiritual discernment requires judgment, but the demonstration of God's love should always be our first consideration. I have a friend in one of my Sunday school classes who told me a story about his grandfather. His grandpa was a quiet, Christian man who kept most of his opinions to himself, but my friend's grandmother was different. She was a tough lady who always knew what line she was in and was very vocal about it.

My friend's grandparents had a neighbor who was prone to drink. Every Saturday night he would run his truck into the ditch and then go to grandpa's house for help. Grandpa never failed to help, but every Sunday morning as they prepared to go to church, grandma would lecture grandpa, reminding him that drinking was a sin and that he should refuse to help the drunken neighbor the next time.

One Sunday morning after being up late again helping his neighbor out of the ditch, grandpa had heard enough lecture and responded, "I don't want to hear any more of this, Grandma. I am not responsible for why my neighbor is in the ditch, but I am responsible for helping him out of it!"

Grandpa was a heart of wisdom Christian. He knew that being a Christian is more than knowing the rules and going to church. Grandpa was applying the expanded version of the Law that Jesus demonstrated with his life – the big picture of God's kingdom.

Jesus brought us a new perspective of God and bridged the gap from the Old Testament to the New Testament. His simple message was based on three absolute spiritual principles: God's love, God's forgiveness, and God's grace. Jesus brought these principles to each of us individually through the righteousness of the law and the fears of the crowd.

When Jesus was confronted by the intellectual experts and the belligerent crowd about the woman who had been caught in sin, He communicated this message: *Thanks for reminding me of the Law, but God loves this woman as much as He loves you, He forgives her as much as he forgives you, and He extends His grace to her just like He does for you.*

The Law was "collectively" understood by the crowd, but Jesus taught them a lesson about love that is timeless. God's love is first extended to us "individually," and that is the simple message.

If you want to be a heart of wisdom Christian, you must understand God loves you, God forgives you, and God extends His grace to you. He does the same for me, too, and for all of us individually; His grace extends to all mankind. That has been a revelation for me and is all the theology I need.

The next time someone wants to read you the rule book on theology or tries to convince you that you must be in the line of some cause, do not be confused. Jesus made it very simple for us because He knew that some would always miss the point and insist on being God's umpires, always calling balls and strikes for others. He also knew that mankind would sometimes misinterpret the demonstration of His love.

There are two questions you can ask yourself to always make sure you are focused on the simple message of Jesus: 1) Do I love before I judge? 2) Do I focus on my own sin before I judge the sin of others?

In Psalms 90:12, the psalmist prayed for God to grant him the ability to number his days correctly so that he may gain a heart of wisdom. We normally think of wisdom as being a product of the head rather than the heart, but the psalmist knew wisdom of the heart only comes to those who seek it. God weighs the heart (Proverbs 21:2), and He values and places priority on the spiritual condition of our heart's intent. The psalmist knew that a head full of knowledge would not bring him to God. He prayed for a heart of wisdom because he knew that the spiritual journey from the head to the heart is the greatest challenge of life.

There are many issues facing the Christian community today, sensitive issues with good Christians on both sides and many in the middle. With most of these issues, neither side is completely right or completely wrong. This dilemma is confusing for many, and confusion leads to division. Confusion also sends a hypocritical message to those who are searching for God. They stand on the perimeter of the contemporary Christian scene and look in. When they see division and confusion, God's simple message of love, forgiveness, and grace is rendered ineffective and misinterpreted as hypocrisy.

Sometimes it seems easier to follow the self-proclaimed experts in the crowd, but that is not what God wants us to do. His love is first extended to us individually, and His greatest desire is to have a close connection with each of us – a personal, individual relationship. God does not require us to have all the answers to life's difficult questions. He simply wants us to rest in His love and gain a heart of wisdom.

Application and Action

Day One: Are there any contemporary Christian issues where you see two lines forming? How will you decide your spiritual position on these issues?

Day Two: Intellectual debate never leads to spiritual truth. Do you agree or disagree? Why?

Day Three: Identify three ways a heart of wisdom Christian benefits the Christian community. How does your response relate to your own behavior?

Day Four: In what ways can you number your days correctly and gain a heart of wisdom?

Day Five: God speaks to each of us. Be sure to keep a journal. Write a brief summary of your spiritual insights and thoughts from this week's lesson.

Lesson Eight:
I Pushy Blue

Focus Point:

God teaches us how to make good
choices through the influence of others
and through trial and error.

Scriptural Foundation:

*It is written in the Prophets: 'They will
all be taught by God.' Everyone who
listens to the Father and learns from
[H]im comes to me.*

John 6:45

I Pushy Blue

I was playing a game with my granddaughter Lilly one evening and learned a great lesson about choices and human nature. It was an electronic game that played musical notes as we pushed different colored lights. However, if we touched the red light, the game would end. To restart the game, we would have to push the green light. Lilly was almost two years old and convinced that she was an expert at this game. Every time the game would end I would say, "Now, Lilly, if you push green, the game will come back on." With a defiant look of determined independence, she would consistently respond, "I pushy blue."

With the push of the blue button nothing would happen, and she would respond with the same sad face of disappointment. On one hand you have to admire Lilly's independent resolve, but the negative result of pushing the wrong button never changed, no matter how determined her resolve.

Our human natures are like that; doing it our way is sometimes more important than getting it right. What end can we possibly serve if, in the light of knowing what is right, we insist on our own solution, even when it is wrong? Lilly reminded me of the many times in my life when I insisted on doing it my way, even when I knew my way was wrong. How many times in my life had I said, "I pushy blue," to important life-lessons?

I pray for my grandchildren everyday. Lilly was my first, and for some time I struggled with what I should ask God to do for Lilly. From experience I know that the quality of her life will depend on the choices she makes, so my prayer for Lilly and my other two grandchildren is simple: *God, send people of great influence in the life-path of Lilly, Thompson, and Mary Liese.*

The Bible says, "They will all be taught by God." I certainly assume that includes my grandchildren, but how can God teach them when they have these independent "I pushy blue" human natures? He teaches them by placing people of great influence in their lives at just the right time.

Think back on your own life. How many people of influence can you identify as God-sends? I am talking about people who influenced you in your most desperate moments. Some may recall one while others may recall many, but whether it is one or one hundred consider this: They were placed in your life by God at the right time and in the right place.

I can think of many people in my life who have positively influenced my choices. My mother, father, brother, teachers, coaches, pastors, my wife, Mary, and my daughters Lauren and Jenni have all influenced my choices for good. I know that God placed them in my life at just the right time.

I have come to see everyday life events as spiritual training ground, and when people move in and out of my life, I understand it is not random or accidental. God influences our choices by people of influence who are placed in our lives. I know that God is preparing some wonderful people to intersect with the lives of my grandchildren at just the right time and place.

Another way God influences our choices is through practical and sometimes difficult trial and error. I cannot number the times I have tried something that did not work. In fact, my greatest lessons have come from trying and failing. The way God influences our future choices through trial and error is by providing us a brain to remember the things that do not work. I know that sounds easy, but the old "I pushy blue" human nature of ours keeps pushing the same buttons regardless of the results.

I know people who seem to make the same mistakes over and over again. God intends for us to truly learn from our life lessons. Think of your own life. How many times have you missed the opportunity to learn from your life lessons? Making the same mistakes over and over again does not move us forward in life. God gave us the capacity to use common sense when it comes to lessons learned. If we make a mistake, we are to truly learn from that mistake and, as a result, not make the same mistake again.

For example, if you have a certain behavior in your life that causes you to be insensitive to others, keeping you from establishing lasting relationships, stop pushing that button. Find someone you can trust who will be honest with you about the things you really need to hear. Learn from the feedback of a trusted friend; stop being defensive about the things in your life that do not work, and start pushing the right buttons. If you are insecure, addicted, compulsive, untrustworthy, unlovable, disappointed, discouraged, arrogant, conceited, or filled with guilt, stop pushing those buttons. God intended us to live effective lives of abundance (John 10:10). Stop saying, "I pushy blue," when blue is not getting you anywhere.

I ask God to influence my grandchildren through His Spirit in a way that will cause them to learn necessary lessons from their inevitable trial and error. They will make mistakes, but with God's guidance they will develop common sense that will negate that old "I pushy blue" human nature. Common sense from God's guiding light will allow them to learn to push the right buttons and live effective lives of abundance.

I was watching an interview in which Oprah Winfrey was asked about the most influential person in her life. She quickly responded that it was her fifth grade school teacher. This person showed her a love that was both touching and encouraging, and Oprah went as far as to say that it was this fifth grade teacher who inspired her to excellence at a particularly difficult time in her life.

That statement has stuck with me for some time, and I have often asked questions about her special teacher: *What if she had not been ready? What if she had a bad attitude? What if she had an insufficient education? What if she was not receptive to God's call? What if she did not have a caring heart? What if she was just having a bad day?*

"What if" was not the case; she was ready. She obviously knew that the only obstacle keeping her from being what God wanted her to be for Oprah was herself. This unassuming fifth grade teacher was ready to assume the role of great influence in the life of a seemingly insignificant little girl who would grow up into a position of great influence. That is how God works! He has people ready to be of great influence at the right place and time. Now for the *real* question: Are you ready to assume your role of influence?

When we connect with God, He starts us on a journey to be placed in a position of great influence for someone, and it usually happens when we least expect it. The event, the person, and the influence may seem insignificant at the time. We may never know the impact of our lives on someone else, but we all need to be ready at the right place and time to be an influence for good in the life of another (1 Peter 3:15).

Yes, Lilly taught me a great lesson about choices and human nature that evening. Now every time I find myself insisting on my own way or using an old solution that I know does not work, I have her words ringing in my ear: "I pushy blue."

Application and Action

Day One: Can you identify any mistakes or unproductive behavior that seems to be reoccurring in your life? If so, what actions will you take to improve or correct them?

Day Two: A famous management consultant, Peter Drucker, defines effectiveness as "Doing more of what works, abandoning what doesn't, and knowing the difference." How can you apply this lesson in effectiveness to your life?

Day Three: Can you identify any "buttons" in your life that you keep pushing, even though they do not work? If yes, what actions will you take to improve or correct your behavior?

Day Four: Make a list of the names of people who have been of great influence in your life. How can you be ready to be of great influence for someone when God needs you?

Day Five: God speaks to each of us. Be sure to keep a journal. Write a brief summary of your spiritual insights and thoughts from this week's lesson.

Lesson Nine: Looking for Grace

Focus Point:

Grace is the foundation of our relationship with God, but we must personally experience it to understand it.

Scriptural Foundation:

But Noah found grace in the eyes of the Lord.

Genesis 6:8 (KJV)

Looking for Grace

What will be the most profound, significant decision of your life?

When we consider all of our life decisions, identifying the most profound is difficult; it is so difficult that we may choose to spend a lifetime ignoring the question altogether. Noah is a familiar Bible character who, when faced with a significant life decision, found God's grace.

Noah built a large boat on dry land in preparation for a cataclysmic flood. Why? God told him to do so. His contemporaries mocked him, his family questioned him, and I am sure there were moments of self-doubt; yet, he completed the impossible mission. Some consider his mission the necessary link in the perpetuation chain of humanity. Without Noah all of mankind and most of the animal kingdom could have been wiped out by the great flood. From a physical perspective, some assume his actions were performed and his significant decisions were made for the good of mankind. However, according to the Bible, Noah found grace, and that was the beginning of the boat project (Genesis 6:8-9). If Noah found grace, he must have been looking for it.

I am not sure he was actually *looking* for grace, but Noah was acting from a spiritual motive. He was going about his daily routine when he heard God call. The Bible tells us that God chose Noah because he was a man who recognized his spiritual connection with God (Genesis 6:9). He conducted his daily affairs by a value system which reflected his relationship with God. At the root of his moral value system was his most profound and significant life decision – his connection with God. At some point in his life, he decided that spiritually connecting with God was a good idea. From that life decision, Noah found God's grace.

Grace is the foundation of our relationship with our Creator. Our humanness inspires us to the physically tangible, but God's grace endears us to Him. The world tends to block our view of God, but God's grace magnifies our vision of Him. We are mere mortals outside the light of God's grace. For that reason, it is God's grace that seals our relationship with Him. What is grace? Unmerited favor.

For example, if your credit card company called you tomorrow and said it was eliminating your debt without requiring you to pay off the balance, that would be unmerited favor. You did not deserve such favor, but you got it. There is, however, one requirement – you must accept the offer.

God covers all of us with His unmerited favor, canceling all our debt (failures and mistakes), but we must choose to accept it. God will not extend His grace beyond our freedom to choose.

There is an old theological joke that starts with a conversation between God and Adam. God said, "Adam, since you are the first of my new creation, I have some good news and some bad news. The good news is you have freedom of choice. The bad news is you have freedom of choice." This joke describes a humorous reality. Free will is God's gift to mankind, but the flip-side of free will is personal responsibility for the consequences of our choices.

Why did God grant mankind the freedom to choose? Consider a guest in your home. Would you want a houseguest living with you who did not want to be there? Your guest would be resentful of your presence, always thinking about being elsewhere, and constantly complaining about the cooking. This example may be simplistic, but it gets to the point of the issue: Choice and freedom are interdependent; one cannot exist without the other. God wants His creation to be free. That is why our American founders defined freedom as an unalienable right endowed by our Creator. Freedom cannot exist without choice, and choice cannot exist without freedom. Therefore, if God's creation is to be free, it must also have the freedom to choose.

God's greatest desire is for mankind to choose His unmerited favor – His grace. However, since mankind is vested with the freedom to choose, some choose to live life alone under the illusion of their own power. It is an illusion because the power of life resides with its

Creator (Psalms 8:3-5). Jesus said he came to bring us a more abundant life (John 10:10).

Okay, we know what grace is, and we know the importance of accepting it, but what does grace do? How does God's grace benefit mankind? The Bible speaks of three kinds of grace: saving grace (Acts 15:11; Ephesians 2:5), abounding grace (2 Corinthians 9:8), and enabling grace (Acts 14:3).

Saving grace meets us at the point of our need. The old hymn "Just As I Am" is a perfect description of this need. We do not have to be perfect to receive this grace. The reality is we are all entrenched in our humanness, which inspires our separation from God, but God's saving grace meets us where we are without any excuse or any need for one. God meets us with His unmerited favor; His saving grace is extended to all those who choose to accept it.

Abounding grace is described in the Bible with this scripture: "And God is able to make all grace abound to you, so that in all things, at all times, having all you need, you will abound in every good work" (2 Corinthians 9:8). Imagine having all you need to live abundantly through all of life's situations. The story of the miracle money told in lesson two is a vivid example of the power of God's abounding grace, and I have personally witnessed and experienced it.

Enabling grace equips us with spiritual power to do God's will. The way God confirms His grace for us is by enabling us to perform beyond our known capabilities (Acts 14:3). This is confirmed through His enabling grace. If you want a grand demonstration of enabling grace, read Acts Chapter 14. Paul and Barnabas came to trust God's enabling grace when they were given power to do "wondrous signs and miracles." When God asked me to write this book, my first response was, "But I don't know how!" God has confirmed His grace for me by enabling me to do something that I truly believe was beyond my personal capabilities before I started.

Yes, Noah indeed found grace in the eyes of the Lord. That grace met him at the level of his need, with all the resources required, and enabled him beyond his personal capabilities to complete a miraculous boat project. That same grace which Noah found is available to all mankind today. Jesus has already paid your fee (1 Peter 3:18). It is free for the asking, but you have to exercise your freedom to choose and accept it. Some may say it cannot be that easy, but it is. Your connection and personal relationship with God is automatic when you ask God to be a part of your moment by moment life. All you have to do is ask God to be the real and powerful center of your life.

Over twenty years ago, I asked God to reveal Himself in my daily life; He has responded with real and powerful life lessons. I now find God's hand in every common event. It is difficult to find a single moment of my day that is outside the influence of God. That is not a testimony to my perfection, for I am still human with all my flaws, but God transforms me beyond my human capabilities through His wonderful grace.

Application and Action

Day One: Noah found grace (favor) in God's eyes. In what ways is God's grace the same today as when Noah found it? In what ways is it different? How does this understanding apply to you?

Day Two: Do you personally view free will (choice) as a benefit or a liability? Name one attitude you could change or action you could take that would increase your benefits of free will and minimize your liabilities. How will you act on this insight?

Day Three: Why is your acceptance of God's grace so important to your personal relationship with Him? How will you respond to this insight?

Day Four: Write a brief paragraph describing what you will do with God's grace.

Day Five: God speaks to each of us. Be sure to keep a journal. Write a brief summary of your spiritual insights and thoughts from this week's lesson.

Lesson Ten:
Seeds of Defeat

Focus Point:

Prosperity is sometimes more difficult
to manage than adversity.

Scriptural Foundation:

Trust in the Lord with all your heart
and lean not on your own understanding;
in all your ways acknowledge [H]im,
and [H]e will make your paths straight.

Proverbs 3:5-6

Seeds of Defeat

Be careful that your victories do not bring with them the seeds of future defeat.

— Unknown

*A*fter hearing this opening quote one Sunday morning, a member of my class gave us all a history lesson. He said that when any of the conquering heroes of the Roman army rode their chariots in the parade celebrating a great military victory, there was always a designated person riding in the chariot directly behind the hero whispering, "Accolades and celebration are fading glory." The purpose of this custom is obvious; the Romans wanted to make sure their military leaders never brought the seeds of future defeat back with them.

How many Hollywood stars can you think of who, after rising to the top, literally self-destruct? I recently witnessed, along with millions of other fans, NBA basketball icons going into the stands and fighting the very fans who had paid to see their professionalism. Seeds of future defeat?

A friend told me about someone he had counseled and supported through some difficult financial times. That person later landed a windfall and became a mega millionaire. My friend called to congratulate him but could not get through or even receive a return call. Seeds of future defeat?

Think of a person who, in your opinion, is truly successful. Now think of one word that describes that person. I have used this exercise before, and the word most often thought of is *humility*. One would think that word would be *drive*, *ambition*, or *hard work*, but that is not so, for it seems obvious that humility and long-term success go hand in hand. Notice that I said "long-term" success. Accolades and material possessions are fading glory. What all of us need is lasting success.

When asked to think of specific seeds of defeat, one usually thinks of pride, self-destructive behavior, haughtiness, arrogance, and so on – all the normal self-defeating behaviors of temporal success. However, one of the most common self-destructive seeds of defeat is complexity. Life seems to happen at an ever increasing pace today. With material and performance-related success come complexities, such as legal issues, tax liabilities, financial planning, and all the ego enhanced temptations. These things create heavy, life-draining complexity.

Complexity leads us away from the abundant life of which Jesus spoke and contradicts the fruit of the Spirit which is love, joy, peace, patience, kindness, goodness, gentleness, faithfulness, and self-control (Galatians 5:22-23). Complexity robs us of our focus on what matters most, causing us to obsess over self and lose our perspective of others.

Please do not be quick to assume that my intent in this lesson is to deride the "evils" of wealth and success, for I believe God desires and plans for us all to be successful, having more than we need (Jeremiah 29:11-12), but there are two distinctly different ways of success – the way of the world and God's way. How do we handle prosperity God's way? How do we balance our lives with abundance and avoid the fog of complexity? I have observed that prosperity is sometimes more difficult to manage than adversity. I suggest six guidelines from the Bible for managing prosperity.

Number one, recognize the source (John 3:27 and James 1:17). The Bible tells us that all good things come from God. Why is it so important to God that we not take credit for our successes? When we take the credit for our successes, we become egocentric, focusing on self. Egocentrism leads to false pride, and pride precedes a fall (Proverbs 16:18). How many times have you watched a top-ranked athletic team get beat by an inferior opponent because they were focused on how good they were rather than on doing their best? God knows that pride in self leads to all kinds of maladies. When we focus on our successes as gifts from God, we take the spotlight off of self. This attitude leads us to always wanting to do our best.

Number two, live with a thankful heart (1 Thessalonians 5:16-18). I cannot explain it, but there is great power in thanksgiving. The act of living with a thankful heart is just a healthy way to live. For example, a member of my church pulled me aside one Sunday and shared how learning to live with a thankful heart had changed her life. She was dealing with a troubled teen and an almost intolerable relationship with her husband. She told me that many nights she just could not see the point in living. Her mind was fixed on all her problems. She never told me why, but she decided to change her thinking process. Rather than focusing on her problems, she began to systematically list all the things for which she was thankful. This was a physical list that she kept as a record, and she added to that list at least one thing each night before she went to bed. She admitted that some days coming up with even one thing was difficult, and sometimes it would be something as simple as a cool evening breeze, but she learned that no matter how bad her problems were, she could always find one thing for which she could be thankful.

This action step developed into a habit of thought. Her thinking process changed from looking for problems to looking for things for which to be thankful. She said that this change in thinking completely transformed her life. That was many years ago, and today she is happy, stable, and most of her old problems are solved. There is power in learning to live with a thankful heart in bad times or good times.

Number three, be committed to integrity (Psalms 15:4). WorldCom and Enron are just two examples of good plans which turned bad. There is no long-term success without integrity, and integrity goes deeper than just good intentions. I have difficulty believing the leadership of these companies set out with the intentions of defrauding anyone. I believe they had good intentions of everyone benefiting, but when profits went south, they devised a plan to boost those profits by hiding expenses or running with the money. That may have never been their initial intent, but that is the very point of real integrity. When an organization's integrity is based on good intentions, success will always be at risk.

With individual or corporate success, integrity must be the foundation of all our efforts. Good intentions, no matter how sincere, are self-serving and tend to bend with situations and circumstances. Success God's way requires integrity that is built on commitment, and He will endorse the success of those who are committed to integrity – no matter what.

Number four, seek simplicity (Matthew 6:32-33). Maybe I am just getting older, but it seems that keeping life simple and uncluttered is becoming more and more difficult. Any successful football coach will tell you that a simple game plan is far more effective than a complex game plan. It is not the number of plays the team can run; it is the number of plays the team can execute effectively. Our life is the same way – the simpler the lifestyle the greater the rewards. Jesus taught us not to chase after the material but to seek His Kingdom first. He added that our Father in Heaven already knows what we need to be successful; therefore, we are to focus on seeking God first and everything else will be added. Simplicity is seeking God first.

Number five, focus on others (Matthew 22:39). I was discussing this topic with an old friend and Christian role model one day when he said something that has stuck with me for years: "You can't get to heaven unless you take your brother with you." I certainly would not open this comment to theological debate, but it makes a lot of sense to me. Think about it. We are not random accidents of nature; we are spiritual beings in physical form placed on earth by our Creator for a reason and purpose. It makes sense that we are all connected in this earthly journey. Why else would Jesus have instructed us to love each other as we love ourself? Success brings dramatic focus on self, and that is contrary to God's plan. We hear that our current times represent the "me" generation where everyone looks out for number one and gets theirs first. But when it comes to success God's way, each of us must always remember… it is not about me; it is about us.

Number six, remember your beginnings (Isaiah 51:1). I came from the other side of the tracks, literally. During my early childhood, my family lived in Riverside, a small section of our hometown in South Carolina. To get to our home you literally had to cross the railroad tracks.

It was a tough neighborhood, and on a recent visit, I had an occasion to take my two daughters on a tour of Riverside. As we crossed the tracks, my oldest daughter, Lauren, said, "Daddy, this is spooky." Then Jenni, my youngest, said, "Let's get out of here!" Yes, my old neighborhood has been overcome with poverty and neglect. It has declined significantly in fifty years, but to tell the truth, it was not much better then. However, I look back to those early years with pride. I came from humble beginnings, and I never want to forget that.

Regardless of the economic conditions of each of our beginnings, they are indeed beginnings. With prosperity comes the tendency to forget our beginnings, when we were insecure and unproven, but remembering our beginnings keeps our perspective clear. Our attention is focused on how thankful we are rather than on how great we are.

A healthy self-image is God's desire for us all, but there is value in remembering our beginnings. It brings prosperity into perspective and reminds us of our obligation to remember those who helped us along the way and to give back to those who can benefit from our success.

Success God's way leads to abundance, and abundance is more than just having tangible things. It includes all the intangible benefits of our connection with God. The Bible refers to those benefits as "fruit of the Spirit" (Galatians 5:22-23). Success God's way is filled with the abundance of love, joy, peace, patience, kindness, goodness, gentleness, faithfulness, and self-control. This abundant life is the only road to lasting success.

Application and Action

Day One: List any potential seeds of defeat you can identify in your own life. What attitudes can you change or actions can you take to reduce one item from this list?

Day Two: List any distracting complexities in your life. What attitudes can you change or actions can you take to reduce one item from this list?

Day Three: Which of the six guidelines for success would hold the most potential for improving your current life position? Why? How will you act on this insight?

Day Four: Write a brief statement defining what true, long-term success is for you personally.

Day Five: God speaks to each of us. Be sure to keep a journal. Write a brief summary of your spiritual insights and thoughts from this week's lesson.

Lesson Eleven: Ya Gotta Go to Know

Focus Point:

God's power is most effective when, by faith, His children call into being that which is not yet seen.

Scriptural Foundation:

Therefore I tell you, whatever you ask for in prayer, believe that you have received it, and it will be yours.

Mark 11:24

Ya Gotta Go to Know

*H*ave you ever been spiritually disappointed? Not with God, but with loved ones who have become spiritually confused? The confusion usually comes from some misunderstanding of scripture or well-meaning friend saying the wrong thing at the wrong time. Your disappointment is not with the person but with the turmoil you see him or her going through.

One of the most spiritually disappointing experiences for me personally was watching a very close friend go through the discouragement of what she interpreted as unanswered prayer. She told me that she had prayed for God to bless her with a grandchild, but that prayer had not been answered. She went on to explain that through a Bible study group, she had been introduced to a scripture in the book of Matthew where the author records the words of Jesus: "Ask and it will be given to you…" (Matthew 7:7). She expressed with deep sadness, "I have asked, and it did not happen." Her reasoning was taking her to a position of spiritual disbelief. Out of discouragement and confusion she asked, "How can I continue to believe when the promises and words of Jesus do not deliver?"

Have you ever counseled someone who was spiritually discouraged? You want to help, but sometimes you just do not know what to say. I have heard some intelligent, well-articulated comments intended to help which ended up doing more harm than good. People who are spiritually disappointed and confused need real answers, and real answers only come from real experience. I am talking about real, personal experience with God's love, promises, and power.

I never attempt intellectual persuasion with someone who is spiritually confused or disappointed. Why? Because we must personally experience spiritual answers before we can ever intellectually understand them. I heard a friend use a catchy, down-home phrase which gives a great description of this concept: "Ya gotta go to know." What does that mean? It is a memorable phrase describing a deeper concept of experience preceding understanding.

Spiritual understanding is developed in complete reverse of the process required for intellectual understanding (1 Corinthians 3:19-20). For example, from an intellectual perspective, we must have knowledge and understanding before we can accept the answers. But from a spiritual perspective, we must personally experience and accept the answers before we can intellectually understand them.

Ya gotta go to know.

There is a distinct difference between intellectual learning and spiritual understanding. When the intellectual learning process is misapplied to attempts at gaining spiritual understanding, many people become confused or disappointed. They reason, *If I can intellectually understand this spiritual issue, then I can accept it.* Personal experience leads me to believe that the reverse is true: *When I accept this spiritual concept by faith, God will grant me experience to help me intellectually understand it.* The Bible itself indicates that the process of gaining spiritual understanding is reverse of the process for gaining intellectual understanding (2 Timothy 2:7). How then are we to develop reassuring spiritual understanding? Through the exercise of faith.

Intellectually we cannot accept anything that we cannot understand. Spiritually we cannot understand anything that we cannot first accept by faith. The one action that sets in motion our spiritual understanding is the exercise of our faith. Notice that I said the "exercise" of our faith; faith is just an empty word unless it is put into action (James 2:17). Our faith is far more than a distinguishing word defining our religious or denominational affiliation; it is the fuel for our spiritual motors. Faith releases God's power here on earth, and it is the teacher of spiritual understanding. "Now faith is being sure of what we hope for and certain of what we do not see" (Hebrew 11:1). Intellectually the concept of faith is nonsensical, but spiritually faith is the key to understanding.

We can apply these same concepts to my friend who was spiritually discouraged and confused over her seemingly unanswered prayer. She learned to read in the first and second grades. She began to comprehend what she was reading in the fourth and fifth grades, so she has been reading for intellectual understanding most of her life. She was introduced to a verse of scripture in the Bible and intellectually understood what the words were saying. Being a new Bible student, she applied the only process for learning she knew: the intellectual process. Remember, using the intellectual process to gain spiritual understanding usually leads to confusion.

Now for the rest of the story, even though she was confused, discouraged, and tempted with disbelief, she began to believe in her hope of answered prayer (Hebrews 6:8-19). She began to speak of things not seen as if they were (Romans 8:24-25). With each small act of faith, her faith grew even stronger, and in God's perfect timing, she became the proud grandmother of six wonderful grandchildren. From that powerful experience of acting on her faith, she has experienced God's power and love in a way that brings spiritual understanding. That spiritual understanding, personally experienced, now makes sense to her intellectually. We must take the bold step of faith to gain spiritual understanding.

Ya gotta go to know.

Now, I need to stop here and deal with the obvious questions: *Why aren't all prayers answered? What if my friend had applied all the faith she could muster and still not had any grandchildren? How much faith does it take?* These are logical questions that anyone may ask. I have asked them myself.

For example, I have a very close friend who told me that when his mother was dying of cancer, he asked God to let her live, but she died. My friend still thinks that God let him down. For years I asked God to explain to me why some prayers are answered and some are not. With time and personal experience, God has led me with three different scriptures to a spiritual understanding of this puzzling issue of unanswered prayer. The first is found in Isaiah 55:8-9 which says that God's thoughts are higher than our thoughts. We cannot possibly comprehend the mind of God. It would stand to reason that since God is the Creator of the universe and of mankind, there are probably many things about eternal issues of timing that we cannot comprehend.

Small children need supervision because they do not comprehend dangers that exist, such as a busy street and walking in the road. They are not intellectually capable of managing their own best interest. A young boy may want to play in the street, but when a loving adult grabs him by the arm and pulls him back to safety, he feels he is not getting what he wants. In much the same way, we ask God for things and circumstances that may not fit in the big scheme of things, and when we do not get what we want, we reason that God did not answer our request. In spiritual reality, God has answered our prayer in a way that is best for us, but it is beyond our understanding.

The second scripture is found in Romans 8:28. This is a promise from God that says no matter what happens, He will work all things together for good for those who love Him and are called according to His purpose. This is my reassurance from God to ask without doubt because I cannot lose. As I trust God to work things together for good, I do not have to worry about how the prayer is answered. God has promised me that He will work all things to my best interest from His perspective. From personal experience I have learned that God's plan for me is better than anything I could possibly plan for myself.

The third scripture is found in Philippians 4:6-7. It tells us not to worry but to allow the peace of God, which transcends all understanding, to guard our hearts and our minds in Christ Jesus. Many times we ask God for things or special circumstances that we think we need, when what we really need is His peace. I cannot verbalize how wonderful it is for me to simply rest in His peace.

If you question stepping out in faith with your prayers, lean on these promises from God because all prayers are answered – maybe not in a way that intellectually makes sense, but always in God's perfect wisdom and timing.

From personal experience with these three scriptures, I have the spiritual understanding needed to encourage myself to pray and ask in faith without doubt. At times it may seem that I am not getting my prayers answered, but I know, in spiritual reality, I am receiving perfect answers to my prayers.

Asking without doubt is an exercise of faith, and the most powerful prayer is when, by faith, we call into being that which is not yet seen. When we live by faith in God's guidance and ask Him for things that we need, we can ask without doubt, knowing that we will receive according to God's wisdom and our best interest. This lifestyle may not seem logical until you have personally experienced it because… Ya gotta go to know.

Application and Action

Day One: Read Mark 11:20-24. Did Jesus exaggerate the example of the mountain falling into the sea to teach us a lesson? What lesson could that be? How does this insight apply to you?

Day Two: What have you learned from this lesson that will help you say the right thing to a spiritually confused or disappointed friend?

Day Three: What spiritual understanding have you gained from personal experience? What actions will you take to expand this understanding?

Day Four: After studying this lesson, how will you respond when you are asked to pray for a mountain-moving miracle?

Day Five: God speaks to each of us. Be sure to keep a journal. Write a brief summary of your spiritual insights and thoughts from this week's lesson.

Lesson Twelve:
The Wind of the Spirit

Focus Point:

God's spiritually transforming work
in us is also the revelation of
His will for us.

Scriptural Foundation:

The wind blows wherever it pleases.
You hear its sound, but you cannot tell where
it comes from or where it is going. So it is with
everyone born of the Spirit.

John 3:8

The Wind of the Spirit

Can you describe the wind? I can describe the feeling of a gentle gust of wind against my face on a hot summer day or the sound of the wind blowing through the leaves of a tall cottonwood tree. I can describe the effects of the wind, but I have real difficulty describing the tangible contents or origin of the wind.

In the original Greek and Hebrew texts of the Bible, the word for *spirit* is the same word used for *wind*, and many of the biblical writers used the example of the wind to enhance their descriptions of the Holy Spirit. Jesus used the example of the wind to help one of the religious leaders of His time understand the concept of the Holy Spirit (John 3:1-21). Nicodemus was a man of the Pharisees and a member of the Jewish ruling council. He came to visit Jesus after dark one evening to have what he thought was going to be a light conversation with an interesting character. Little did he know that he was about to have a life-changing encounter with the Son of God.

Jesus told Nicodemus that physical birth is the obvious transport to life here on earth, but one must be spiritually born again to see the kingdom of God (John 3:3). Then Jesus used the wind as an example. He said you cannot physically control, see, or describe the wind, but you can feel the effects of the wind. Jesus then said that the Spirit of God and everyone born of the Spirit is like the wind. Later He said the world cannot see, explain, or accept the Spirit because He (the Spirit) is only understood spiritually (John 14:16-17). One must have a spiritual connection with God (spiritual birth) to benefit from the Spirit's direction.

Nicodemus started with some light conversation, but Jesus went directly to the real question that was held secretly in the mind of Nicodemus: *Can you tell me how God can be real to me like He is to you?* This question cuts to the heart of man's universal search for God. Nicodemus was a Jewish leader and a knowledgeable expert in God's law, but he saw something in Jesus that he himself was missing – the real power of God in his life.

Like Nicodemus, we all want to feel the real effects of God's Spirit in our lives. The search for the "realness" of God is fundamental to mankind. This realness begins with a spiritual relationship with God that goes beyond intellectual understanding, theology, or church membership. This spiritual relationship with God begins a supernatural, spiritual transformation that Jesus described as being similar to birth or being born again. Like the wind, we cannot physically describe this process, but we can sure feel the effects of God's transforming work in us. That spiritual transformation takes place in a supernatural way that is outside the realm of physical sight or intellectual understanding, but it is the key to God being real in our daily living. The wind defies description, but its effects are real.

How do I begin this spiritual transformation? Nicodemus had the same question secretly tucked away in his thoughts when Jesus encouraged him by telling him he must be born again (John 3:3).

Some twenty years ago, someone very close to me began to search for God in a real relationship rather than a superficial, religious context. Having been a regular church member since his childhood, he had drifted into an intellectual relationship with God. God was real only in a belief system based on church membership and intellectual understanding.

After some difficult times that now seem self-induced, he reasoned that either God is real with real power, or all of this religious stuff is a waste. He also reasoned that he could never really know God if he was depending on someone else to interpret God for him. He thought that surely God would light the way to spiritual insight and power if God was really there.

I can describe this person with great insight because this friend is me, and the description is my personal story. From this personal revelation years ago, I began to search for God spiritually. I daily asked God to show me His presence in a real, practical, common sense way. I began to read the Bible with a new spiritual intent. Before reading a chapter each day, beginning in Genesis, I would ask

God to show me what He wanted me to see and understand. As God guided me through the Bible in three readings over five years, I would underline the parts that caught my attention. Little did I know that it was the Holy Spirit guiding me through God's word.

I continued to search for God, and He began to send me life lessons as practical examples of His guidance. After five years of searching for God spiritually, He called me to teach. My only resource or qualification was my practical life lessons and the underlined parts from my Bible study. Many of those underlined parts now serve as the scriptural foundations for *Lessons for a Lifetime*.

The Holy Spirit transformed my intellectual understanding of God into a spiritual, personal relationship with Him. In addition, God put me in the center of His will by first preparing me and then placing me in a teaching position of an adult Sunday school class. Then God called me to write this book. Through my personal spiritual experiences, I have learned that God reveals Himself to each of us at the level of our need. The starting point is accepting God's gift of love, forgiveness, and grace and a commitment to spiritually seek Him. God's spiritually transforming work in us is also the revelation of His will for us.

To better understand this principle and the effects of the Spirit in revealing God's will, consider a sailboat. Sailboats come in all sizes, colors, and designs, but they all have one thing in common – they have no power of their own. They all depend on the wind for power and direction; the wind actually brings a sailboat to life. A sailboat has little value without the wind; the wind transforms the sailboat into a useful, worthy vessel.

Some sailboats have motors that allow them to, at times, ignore the wind and go in any direction they choose. But under the motor's power and influence, the sailboat loses its uniqueness and true identity. A sailboat without the wind is incomplete.

We share some common ground with a sailboat. We come in all sizes and colors, and we are incomplete without the effects of God's Spirit. It is

His Spirit that transforms us into who we were intended to be. So many people spend their lifetime searching for God's will when all they need to do is cast their sails to the wind of God's Spirit. Remember, God's will for our lives is all about the journey, not the destination. Even when placed in the center of God's will, we will always have places to go and people to see. It is all about the journey.

Also, like the sailboat, we come with self-propelled motors – our human natures. We can choose to ignore God's Spirit and cruise through life under our own power; however, we will never find God's will for our lives under our own power and direction. We must remember who we really are. We are His children designed to be directed by the wind of His Spirit. Each day we can choose to crank our motors and go under our own power, or we can choose to cast our sails to catch the wind of God's Spirit. As we are directed by His Spirit, His will for our lives is revealed.

His will for us is about the journey, not the destination, and as we proceed through this journey at the direction of the Holy Spirit, God's will for us is revealed along the way.

Here is to your smooth sailing!

Application and Action

Day One: Read John 3:1-12. List the ways Jesus described the difference between the physical and the spiritual. How does this difference affect your search for the realness of God?

Day Two: In John Chapter 3, Jesus used the term "born again." In what ways is this term instrumental in your personal connection with God?

Day Three: After studying this lesson, how will you seek the realness of God?

Day Four: After studying this lesson, how will you seek God's will for your life?

Day Five: God speaks to each of us. Be sure to keep a journal. Write a brief summary of your spiritual insights and thoughts from this week's lesson.

Reflection and Summary

My sincere prayer for you is that these lessons have, in some way, highlighted a specific area of your spiritual life. God speaks to each of us in unique ways, and I am honored that He may have spoken to you through *Lessons for a Lifetime*.

God gave me the title for this book and called me to write it over four years ago. I struggled with this call for three years before finally deciding to be obedient and pick up a pen and start. It was from this struggle that I received "The Day of Small Things." This is just an example of how all of these lessons were received and presented. I tell you this so that I may lift up God's contributions and discount mine. This is really not *my* book; it is *our* book.

As I reflect on the book's completion, I pray that it is not misconstrued as a testimony to my perfection or righteousness. I am just like you and everyone else – a person with flaws and imperfections who struggles daily with mistakes, questions, and temptation. I can be credited with only one thing: finding God in a real and powerful way, and that is God's blessing more than my capacity.

If you are interested in developing a deeper experience with God, I recommend that you become a seeker. God has promised that if you seek with all your heart, you will find. The operative here is "with all your heart." Be bold in asking God to show Himself to you in real and powerful ways. Do not be timid in asking God to become involved in your moment by moment life. The abundant life that Jesus talked about is composed of ordained moments in which your lessons for a lifetime reside. Also, you are never too old or too young to begin this journey.

You are not an accident. Our Creator placed each of us here with a purpose. But only through a spiritual connection with God can you find your true purpose. I find it difficult to understand why everyone would not choose this abundant journey of purpose. I can only reason some feel that allowing God too close to their daily living would cramp their style or limit their fun; not so, it is exactly the opposite. When we open our lives to God, that is when the fun really starts. We do not have to be anyone but ourselves. God takes us just as we are. We do not have to pretend that we are righteous when we know we are not. We are perfect only through our connection with God. Outside God's amazing grace, we are mere mortals.

I do think it is important to understand that when you choose to allow God to be your partner for life, a transformation will take place. You may not see it in the beginning, and sometimes you will only see progress by looking back, but God will transform you into your unique self, your true identity. One of the first things you will notice is that God will begin to talk to you. Now beliefs differ here, but it only seems spiritually natural that if it is important for us to talk to God, He would want to talk to us.

I had a friend tell me about this transformation in her five-year-old daughter, Alana. This little girl had asked her mother this question time and time again: "If we can talk to God, why does He not talk back?" Alana's parents confirmed to her that God does speak to us but in different ways. Alana's prayers for the next several weeks ended with a bold request: "God, will you talk to me?" After each request, she would conclude, "I still can't hear Him."

After weeks of tenacious petition, one night after finishing her prayer, she omitted her normal request and instead looked up; with an amazing smile, she pointed to her head and exclaimed, "I got it! God puts it in your thinking!" Yes, she got it; God talked back. This five-year-old little girl is only in the beginning of her exciting journey.

Be sure to keep a journal of the things God puts in your thinking. I did this for two years before grasping the significant confirmation that God was talking to me.

Another part of this spiritual transformation is that God will begin to place you according to His purpose, or your purpose; they are the same. He will begin to call you outside your comfort zone and ask you to act on your faith. Remember, small beginnings are significant to God. Never let what you cannot do get in the way of what you can do. Start with what you can do, and trust God with the rest. God will take you places you never thought possible. His enabling grace pushes us beyond our human capacities.

God's will and purpose for your life is always about the journey, not the destination. The abundant life of which Jesus spoke is for today (Hebrews 4:7). God never wants you to put your life on hold waiting for that perfect job, place, or position in life. You are here on earth today for a purpose and a reason. That purpose is to learn to trust God and depend on His guidance through all things. All you need to do is cast your sails to the wind of God's Spirit, and regardless of circumstance, you will find yourself in the center of His will.

May God bless you and your journey.

APPENDIX

Leader's Guide

I am sure there are many creative ways to use this book with groups, and the number of ideas would be limited only by one's imagination. Therefore, I will only suggest a basic format and confirm some of the more proven teaching points.

I believe the most important objective of this book is to stimulate independent thinking. The thought provoking process in *Lessons for a Lifetime* leads each participant to confront his or her own personal relationship with God and experience His power in his or her own life. Spiritual transformation through the work of the Holy Spirit can consistently occur when God is experienced personally in real-life examples that make good common sense.

Another enhanced benefit from these lessons is having those who are true seekers embrace the realness of God, which will guide them into a deeper spiritual experience. I have also observed that the practical life-lessons work well with couples in stimulating discussion during the week about the lessons.

The application and action section at the end of each lesson is designed to stimulate the practical applications and actions required to motivate desirable change. I would be remiss to speak of teaching God's word without emphasizing the influence of the Holy Spirit. Ask God to guide you in your lesson preparations and delivery. My consistent prayer over the years has been this: *God bless my preparations; guide the lesson content, bless my delivery, and let this lesson be something specific for someone.*

In summary, I suggest the following procedure in using this book with Sunday school classes or Bible study groups.

I. Leader Preparation:

> Read the book and read through the application and action sections. Take note of your own personal stories and insights relating to the lessons. You will use these later with the group.

II. Kick-off Lesson (30-45 min.):

> A. Introduce the book and distribute a copy to each person. Ask the group to read the introduction and first lesson before the next group meeting.
>
> B. Explain the application and action section; ask the group to complete all five activities for lesson one and to be prepared to discuss their insights at the next meeting.
>
> C. Encourage the use of a journal to record personal thoughts and insights. God speaks to each of us. Encourage each participant to listen and learn to hear that "voice behind you" (Isaiah 30:21).
>
> D. Explain what will happen each week in class (see item III.)

III. Lessons One Through Twelve (30-45 min. each):

> A. Begin with your own personal stories or insights relating to the lesson (10-15 min.) Bring the lesson to life with your real-life examples. God's most profound lessons come from common, everyday events.

B. Direct a general open discussion relating to the lesson (10-15 min.) It is important that you make everyone feel comfortable and welcome. Confirm to the group that all discussion is voluntary. Speaking out in groups can be intimidating or embarrassing for some.

C. Direct a discussion of the five Application and Actions for the week (10-15 min.) Remind and encourage participants to keep a journal and write down what God "puts in their thinking."

IV. Reflection and Summary:

A. Begin with your own reflections about the book (10-15 min.)

B. Direct a discussion relating to the most important spiritual insight participants gained from their experiences with the book (10-15 min.)

C. Close with a discussion relating to the most significant Application or Action participants will personally apply (10-15 min.)

About the Author

David Byrd is president of Leadership Management, Inc., an international leadership and management development company located in Waco, Texas. He holds a master's degree in education from the University of South Carolina.

He and his wife, Mary, live in Waco and have two grown daughters, two great sons-in-law, and three wonderful grandchildren, with a fourth on the way. David and Mary are members of First United Methodist Church of Waco where he teaches two adult Sunday school classes.

Fifteen years ago, David started teaching with a temporary commitment of six months. From that small start, he continues today as a Sunday school teacher with a mission: to have each member of his classes experience the realness of God. He believes that God called him to teach and has now called him to write this book. To communicate with the author go to www.lessonsforalifetime.com.